HARDLUCKY

by Miriam Chaikin
pictures by Fernando Krahn

Once there was an unlucky man.
So he thought of himself. And so he
was.

If he was near a door, he caught
his finger in it. If near a wall, he
banged his head.

Hardlucky, they called him.

Poor Hardlucky is always in trouble.
Thinking that his hometown is just an
unlucky place to be, he travels in
search of a better life. But his mis-
fortune follows him until one day he
meets an old man to whom he tells
his troubles. The kind old man ex-
plains to Hardlucky that he is not unlucky—just stupid. If only he would
think before he acted, his lot would
improve considerably. Following this
valuable advice, Hardlucky's fortune
does improve, and he returns home at
last to become a success in his work
—making omelettes.

Miriam Chaikin's witty words and
Fernando Krahn's funny pictures add
up to a hilarious picture story which
will engross and delight young
children.

HARDLUCKY

HARDLUCKS

by Miriam Chaikin

pictures by Fernando Krahn

J. B. Lippincott Company / Philadelphia and New York

U.S. Library of Congress Cataloging in Publication Data

Chaikin, Miriam.
Hardlucky.
SUMMARY: Hardlucky learns that he really isn't unlucky, just stupid—and the best cure for that is thinking.
[1. Humorous stories] I. Krahn, Fernando, illus. II. Title.
PZ7.C3487Har   [E]   72-8821   ISBN-0-397-31458-2 (reinforced bdg.)

For Shami (Cinderelli)

Once there was an unlucky man. So he thought of himself. And so he was.

If he was near a door, he caught his finger in it. If near a wall, he banged his head. If there was something on the ground, he stepped in it.

Hardlucky, they called him.

One day Hardlucky's luck was worse than usual. He left his wagon standing on the hill and went to deliver wood. When he got back he found that the wagon had rolled down the hill and hit a cow. Hardlucky was fined by the magistrate, his boss took away the wagon, and Hardlucky was out of a job.

So it went with him. Poor Hardlucky.

He walked home and warmed himself by the fire. After a while he heated up some soup and ate it. Then he took off his shoes and went to sleep.

As he slept, a gust of wind blew down the chimney whipping up the flames. First his shoes caught fire. Then the chair. Before long, Hardlucky was standing in the middle of the road scratching his head and gazing around at the ashes that had been his hut.

"Woe is me," he cried. Not knowing where to go or what to do, he sat down. And sitting, he dozed off.

A blind beggar came walking by and stabbed Hardlucky's foot with his stick. Hardlucky jumped up, grabbed the hurting foot, and began to hop around. As he did so he stepped on the tail of a passing dog. And the dog bit him in the other leg.

There and then Hardlucky decided to leave. His luck was bad here in his home town. Perhaps he would have better luck in another place. So thinking, he collected a few stones to start building a new house with, wrapped them in a bundle, and set out for the river.

He took not the regular road but the goats' road. It was a shortcut but very steep. And he slipped and slid, slipped and slid. When he saw a boat preparing to leave and started to run, he fell and couldn't get up again. He rolled downhill, his bundle bumping along after him, and arrived at the pier in a heap.

"Mate!" the captain cried, looking over the side. "Some fool left two bundles behind. Go get them!"

The mate hurried down and soon returned with two bundles. He placed them both before the captain.

The captain stood dumbfounded as one of the bundles uncurled itself and straightened up to become Hardlucky. Looking Hardlucky in the eye, he demanded to know why he had disguised himself as a bundle. Hardlucky said he hadn't disguised himself. And he went on to explain how he had rolled downhill.

"Liar!" the captain shouted.

He gazed down at the other bundle lying at his feet and walked around it.

"And I suppose you're going to tell me that this is not your traveling companion, but another bundle," he said, and gave the bundle a kick.

The captain broke his toe on the stones in the bundle and ordered Hardlucky arrested.

"Woe is me," Hardlucky cried as they dragged him off.

Day after day Hardlucky sat below. One morning they passed
some land. Two mates came and got Hardlucky and flung him
over the side.

"Good riddance," they cried after him.

Hardlucky found himself in a strange land. He looked around,
wondering where he could be. The place was odd, and odd were
its people. A group of them stood about, watching him. Then one,
the smallest of the lot, came toward him. *A street urchin,*
Hardlucky thought to himself.

The street urchin put out his hand.

"*Dja hav nyk oinz,*" he said, which in the language of the place meant, Welcome.

Hardlucky thought he had asked for coins. He turned his pockets inside out, to show he had none. "I'm sorry," he said.

Instantly, he was seized and thrown into jail.

Ahm sah ri in the language of the place meant, I spit on your land. To make matters even worse, the street urchin was no street urchin at all, but the mayor.

Hardlucky sat in jail, saying nothing and speaking to no one. In the morning he was taken by some guards to the border and shoved over to the other side.

By now, it mattered little to Hardlucky where he was. And it mattered even less where he went. But he couldn't just stand there. He had to move in some direction. So he turned his feet to the right and began to walk. And he walked and walked. When he could walk no more, he sat down near a clump of bushes and put his head in his hands. "Oh, woe is me," he wailed. "Woe! Woe! Woe!"

It happens that on the other side of the bushes an old man was passing on his mule. The old man had been trying for some minutes to bring his mule to a halt. But the mule would not be stopped. Where the old man's kicks and slaps had failed, Hardlucky's voice had succeeded. For at his cry of *Woe!* the mule came to a sudden halt. The old man dismounted and went to look for the source of the voice. He saw Hardlucky on the other side of the bushes and went around to speak to him.

"Thank you for bringing my mule to a halt," he said. "Now I can rest for a moment. But tell me, young man," he added, "why you are so unhappy."

Hardlucky looked up. It had been such a long time since anyone had spoken kindly to him that when he opened his mouth to speak he began to cry instead. And through his tears he told the old man about all his bad luck.

The old man smiled at Hardlucky. "I have good news for you," he said. "You are not unlucky at all."

Hardlucky looked up. "Not unlucky?"

The old man shook his head. "No, only stupid," he said.

Hardlucky blinked.

The old man sat down next to Hardlucky.

Taking Hardlucky by the shoulder he said: "If you had stopped to think, none of those things could have happened to you. If you hadn't put your shoes near the flame, they could not have caught fire. And if you hadn't fallen asleep in the road, the blind man could not have stabbed you. If you had taken the regular road to the river, you would have arrived looking like a person and not like a bundle. As for the stones—why take stones from one place to another? There are plenty of stones everywhere."

The old man nodded in the direction of the border. "What happened over there could have been avoided, too," he said. "If you had paid attention, you would have seen that the urchin was an old man, and you would have noticed that he was speaking a different language."

Hardlucky smiled. "Then I'm not unlucky?"

The old man smiled back. "Pay attention to what you're doing," he said as he rose to his feet. "Stop to think. You will see how your luck will change." He then mounted his mule. "I must be on my way now," he said, and rode off.

Hardlucky was joyous. He began to dance around. He wasn't unlucky, after all. If he paid attention, and he stopped to think, his luck would change. So thinking, he decided to return home.

Once more Hardlucky set out for the river. The old man's words danced in his mind. They made him feel so good, he began to run and jump and skip. Suddenly he tripped and fell. Hardlucky got up. He shook his head as he looked around at all the signs reading, *Do Not Run, Jump, or Skip.* If he had been paying attention, he would have noticed the warning.

Hardlucky promised himself not to forget the old man's words
again. This time he walked carefully, looking this way and that. If
he was drowsy, he pinched himself to keep awake. If he was near
a door, he watched his fingers. If near a wall, he watched his head.
If he saw something on the ground, he stepped around it. So
doing, he arrived safely at the port.

He asked which ships were bound for his home town. And he
went from ship to ship asking for work. "What can you do?" asked
one captain. Hardlucky was about to answer "Nothing." But he
remembered the old man's words. And he stopped to think. If he
said "Nothing," that's what he would get. So he said, "Whatever
needs doing, if someone will show me how."

Hardlucky was taken aboard and put to work in the galley. He was taught first how to candle eggs. Then he was taught how to crack them on the side of a dish. He paid attention and learned well. Soon he could candle eggs along with the best. And crack them without looking.

Hardlucky was then taught how to make a plain omelette. He found it difficult to remember all the steps. But he was determined to succeed. So he memorized them: *Crack, beat, add salt, mix, drop into pan, watch, turn, watch, remove from flame,* he repeated all day long. He recited the steps in his sleep, too. When it came time to make his first omelette, he forgot the salt. But the next time he remembered. And soon he was making jelly omelettes and cheese omelettes and omelettes with fine herbs and even shrimp omelettes. By the time the ship reached his home town, everyone was agreed that Hardlucky had learned how to make the best omelettes that any of them had ever tasted.

As a parting gift, the captain gave Hardlucky a hen. The crew gave him a frying pan. Thinking had become second nature to Hardlucky. And it didn't take him long to figure out what to do next. He took some rocks from along the pier and built a place to cook. He took an old wooden crate, turned it upside down, and called it a table. He made a sign reading OMELETTES. And before the day was out, Hardlucky had opened a restaurant in his own home town.

News of the Hardlucky Omelette spread. The sailors told the
hill people. The hill people told the town people. The restaurant
grew and grew. Soon the Hardlucky Omelette was famous
everywhere around.

They still called him Hardlucky. No one could remember why anymore. Not even Hardlucky himself.

About the Author

Miriam Chaikin was born in Jerusalem and raised in Brooklyn, N. Y., the eldest of five children. Her first job was working for the Jewish underground, trying to seek Israel's freedom in the 1940s. She then worked in Washington for two senators before she started on a career in publishing. Along with editing children's books, Miriam Chaikin has written a number of her own, including *Ittki Pittki, The Happpy Pairr and Other Love Stories,* and *Hardlucky.* Her home is in Greenwich Village.

About the Illustrator

Fernando Krahn, a Chilean, lives in Santiago with his wife and three children. He has written as well as illustrated many books, including *Journeys of Sebastian, How Santa Claus Had a Long and Difficult Journey Delivering His Presents,* and *What Is a Man?* Mr. Krahn, recently awarded a Guggenheim Fellowship, plans to pursue his interest in animated films. His cartoons are seen regularly in the *Atlantic Monthly.*